COLOSSAL CITY COUNT

Illustrated by Andy Rowland

Edited by Jonny Marx

Designed by Jack Clucas

Cover design by Angie Allison and Rachel Lawston

Buster Books

INTRODUCTION

Inspector Metropolis and Constable Magnate are operating undercover on an incredibly important mission. They are trying to track down world-renowned villains in some of the busiest and most vibrant cities on the planet.

Your mission, should you choose to accept it, will take you on a whistle-stop tour of the globe. Can you help the police gather evidence at each crime scene by finding and correctly counting the clues in each city to help them crack the criminal case?

Inspector Metropolis

Constable Magnate

12365

INSTRUCTIONS

1. Each city includes a checklist, showing the items you need to count and boxes to write your answers in.

2. Add up all of your answers. Does your total match the number in the total box that the police wrote down?

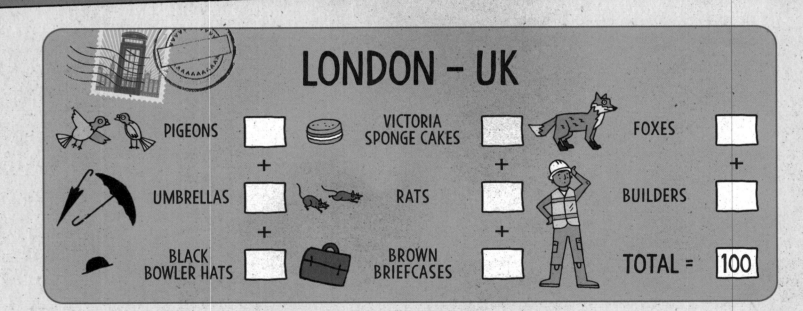

LONDON – UK

PIGEONS	☐	VICTORIA SPONGE CAKES	☐	FOXES	☐
+		+		+	
UMBRELLAS	☐	RATS	☐	BUILDERS	☐
+		+			
BLACK BOWLER HATS	☐	BROWN BRIEFCASES	☐	TOTAL =	100

LONDON – UK

PIGEONS	42	VICTORIA SPONGE CAKES	6	FOXES	6
+		+		+	
UMBRELLAS	5	RATS	9	BUILDERS	14
+		+			
BLACK BOWLER HATS	10	BROWN BRIEFCASES	8	TOTAL =	100

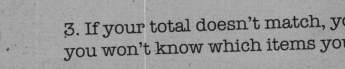

3. If your total doesn't match, you'll have to start again, because you won't know which items you have counted incorrectly!

WANTED

Someone has dropped a passport in every scene. Can you find them all?

There are 18 criminals hiding throughout the book. They all have pet dogs that look a bit like them. Can you find them all and tick them off?

Dave Smith

Dick Dempsey

Lotte Visser

Lord Alfonso

Sophie Moreau

Brad Botha

Chad Nelson

Tarquin Tops

Tommy Chu

Dame Droopy

Evil Bob

Slick McGee

Sam Snoop

Kenneth Cups

Kim Klaws

Cedric Suspense

Cuthbert VI

Lady Jane Grey

You will find all the answers in the back of the book.

There are 18 different locations to explore:

Paris, France
Suzhou, China
Delhi, India
New York City, USA
Amsterdam, Netherlands
Sydney, Australia

Istanbul, Turkey
Moscow, Russia
London, UK
Teotihuacán, Mexico
Cape Town, South Africa
Tokyo, Japan

Berlin, Germany
Venice, Italy
Cairo, Egypt
Barcelona, Spain
Rio de Janeiro, Brazil
Timbuktu, Mali

FROMAGERIE PARFUMERIE

Suzhou – China

Lion statues ☐ + Lifebuoys ☐ + Mandarin ducks ☐ +

Ming vases ☐ + Firecrackers ☐ + Tea pots ☐

Noodle bowls and chopsticks ☐ Yin-Yang symbols ☐ Total = 60

Delhi — India

Peacocks [ ] + Lotus flowers [ ] + White cows [ ] +

Elephant statues [ ] + Sitars [ ] + Macaques [ ]

Cricket bats [ ] + Red saris [ ] + Total = 55

New York City – USA

Peregrine Falcons ☐

Statue of Liberty Ornaments ☐

Basketballs ☐

+

Saxophones ☐

American Football Helmets ☐

Hamburgers ☐

+

Firemen ☐

Raccoons ☐

Total = 50

AMSTERDAM — NETHERLANDS

RADIOS ☐ +	WHEELS OF EDAM CHEESE ☐ +	BUNCHES OF PURPLE TULIPS ☐ +	
RED BICYCLES ☐ +	PAINT PALETTES ☐ +	DUCKS ☐	
HOCKEY STICKS ☐	CUPS OF COFFEE ☐	TOTAL = 80	

Sydney – Australia

🏐 Volleyballs	☐	🐨 Koalas	☐	🦘 Kangaroos	☐
+		+		+	
Didgeridoos	☐	🕊 Seagulls	☐	Meat pies	☐
+		+			
🐢 Turtles	☐	Boomerangs	☐	Total =	70

LONDON – UK

	PIGEONS			VICTORIA SPONGE CAKES			FOXES	
		+			+			+
	UMBRELLAS			RATS			BUILDERS	
		+			+			
	BLACK BOWLER HATS			BROWN BRIEFCASES			TOTAL =	100

TEOTIHUACÁN — MEXICO

AZTEC HEADRESSES	☐	DONKEYS	☐	GREEN SOMBREROS	☐
	+		+		+
COATIS	☐	SNAKES	☐	PIÑATAS	☐
	+		+		
CACTI	☐	RED BALLOONS	☐	TOTAL =	65

Cape Town – South Africa

Rugby balls		Spyglasses		Cape gurnard	
+		+		+	
Vuvuzelas		Tribal masks		Seals	
+		+			
Springboks		Leopard tortoises		Total =	60

CAPE TOURS

CAPE TOURS

Berlin — Germany

Item	Count	Item	Count	Item	Count
Football boots		Tubas		Bratwurst in buns	
	+		+		+
German flags		Televisions		Gramophones	
	+		+		
Goshawks		German shepherd dogs		Total =	50

GALERIE

Trinken Essen

Essen Essen

8 9 10 11 12 13 14

U
Alexanderplatz

Venice – Italy

Busts		Roman vases		Bottles of olive oil		
+		+		+		
Pizzas		Venetian masks		Gondoliers		
+		+				
Ice creams		Holdalls		Total =	55

Barcelona – Spain

Mop & buckets ☐

Swordfish ☐ +

Cordobes hats ☐ +

Binoculars ☐ +

Maps ☐ +

Iberian pigs ☐ +

Bowls of paella ☐

Guitars ☐

Total = 55

GRACIA

PARC GUELL

Rio de Janeiro — Brazil

Tapirs		Footballs		Spotted Frogs	
+		+		+	
Tarantulas		Leopards		Sloths	
+		+			
Flashing Cameras		Stewards		**Total = 60**	

Timbuktu – Mali

Sacks of salt ☐ Baskets of cotton ☐ Nuggets of gold ☐
+
Books ☐ Oryx ☐ Ostriches ☐
+
Vultures ☐ Xylophones ☐ Total = 55

Paris – France

	Pink and black shopping bags	6		Eiffel tower ornaments	5		Blue, white and red scarves	4
Baguettes	4		Watering cans	6		Cats of all breeds	11
Bouquets of red roses	9		Red and black high heels	5		Total =	50

Suzhou – China

	Lion statues	5		Lifebuoys	9		Mandarin ducks	13
Ming vases	7		Firecrackers	6		Tea pots	7
Noodle bowls and chopsticks	8		Yin-Yang symbols	5		Total =	60

Delhi – India

Peacocks	6	Lotus flowers	9	White cows	5
Elephant statues	8	Sitars	6	Macaques	9
Cricket bats	8	Red saris	4	Total =	55

NEW YORK CITY – USA

Peregrine falcons	7	Statue of Liberty ornaments	5	Basketballs	5
Saxophones	6	American football helmets	5	Hamburgers	9
Firemen	6	Raccoons	7	Total =	50

Istanbul – Turkey

Orange lanterns 4 | Seabass 8 | Evil eye necklaces 6
+ | + | +
Mice 22 | Boxes of Turkish delight 8 | Rolled-up Turkish rugs 6
+ | + | +
Turkish teapots 9 | Seagulls 17 | Total = 80

SOUVENIRS
Fancy Goods
RUGS
SPICES
CERAMICS
SOUVEN

MOSCOW – RUSSIA

BAR-HEADED GEESE 7 | SNOW-MOBILES 4 | RED SQUIRRELS 6
+ | + | +
FABERGÉ EGGS 6 | MATRYOSHKA DOLLS 5 | NUTCRACKER FIGURINES 8
+ | + | +
SNOWMEN 5 | ACCORDIONS 4 | TOTAL = 45

сувениры

LONDON – UK

PIGEONS	42	VICTORIA SPONGE CAKES	6	FOXES	6	
+		+		+		
UMBRELLAS	5	RATS	9	BUILDERS	14	
+		+				
BLACK BOWLER HATS	10	BROWN BRIEFCASES	8	TOTAL =	100	

PICCADILLY CIRCUS

TEOTIHUACÁN — MEXICO

AZTEC HEADRESSES	6	DONKEYS	5	GREEN SOMBREROS	10	
+		+		+		
COATIS	9	SNAKES	10	PIÑATAS	6	
+		+				
CACTI	7	RED BALLOONS	12	TOTAL =	65	

Berlin – Germany

Football boots	9	Tubas	5	Bratwurst in buns	7		
+		+		+			
German flags	7	Televisions	5	Gramophones	6		
+		+					
Goshawks	6	German shepherd dogs	5	Total =	50		

Venice – Italy

Busts	5	Roman vases	7	Bottles of olive oil	8
	+		+		+
Pizzas	4	Venetian masks	4	Gondoliers	12
	+		+		
Ice creams	8	Holdalls	7	Total =	55

RIO DE JANEIRO – BRAZIL

Tapirs	3	Footballs	11	Spotted Frogs	13
+		+		+	
Tarantulas	9	Leopards	3	Sloths	6
+		+		+	
Flashing Cameras	12	Stewards	3	Total =	60

Timbuktu – Mali

Sacks of salt	7	Baskets of cotton	4	Nuggets of gold	6
+		+		+	
Books	6	Oryx	6	Ostriches	5
+		+			
Vultures	15	Xylophones	6	Total =	55